OCT -- 2011

JE COLE
Cole, Joanna
The missing

P9-AGM-375

WITHDRAWN

'06 x 6/21 -W
126 x 7/23

Dear Parent:

Congratulations! Your child is taking the first steps on an exciting journey. The destination? Independent reading!

STEP INTO READING® will help your child get there. The program offers five steps to reading success. Each step includes fun stories and colorful art. There are also Step into Reading Sticker Books, Step into Reading Math Readers, Step into Reading Write-In Readers, Step into Reading Phonics Readers, and Step into Reading Phonics First Steps! Boxed Sets—a complete literacy program with something for every child.

Learning to Read, Step by Step!

Ready to Read   Preschool–Kindergarten
• big type and easy words • rhyme and rhythm • picture clues
For children who know the alphabet and are eager to begin reading.

Reading with Help   Preschool–Grade 1
• basic vocabulary • short sentences • simple stories
For children who recognize familiar words and sound out new words with help.

Reading on Your Own   Grades 1–3
• engaging characters • easy-to-follow plots • popular topics
For children who are ready to read on their own.

Reading Paragraphs   Grades 2–3
• challenging vocabulary • short paragraphs • exciting stories
For newly independent readers who read simple sentences with confidence.

Ready for Chapters   Grades 2–4
• chapters • longer paragraphs • full-color art
For children who want to take the plunge into chapter books but still like colorful pictures.

STEP INTO READING® is designed to give every child a successful reading experience. The grade levels are only guides. Children can progress through the steps at their own speed, developing confidence in their reading, no matter what their grade.

Remember, a lifetime love of reading starts with a single step!

To Bartley Jacob, who is just getting his teeth
—J.C.
To Ira & James August
—M.H.

Library of Congress Cataloging-in-Publication Data
Cole, Joanna.
The missing tooth / by Joanna Cole ; illustrated by Marylin Hafner.
  p. cm. — (Step into reading. A step 3 book.)
SUMMARY: Best friends Arlo and Robby are almost identical in what they
wear, what they like, and even where they have teeth missing, but when
Robby insists on betting on who is going to lose the next tooth, their
friendship is endangered.
ISBN 0-394-89279-8 (trade) — ISBN 0-394-99279-2 (lib. bdg.)
[1. Friendship—Fiction. 2. Teeth—Fiction.] I. Hafner, Marylin, ill.
II. Title. III. Step into reading. Step 3 book. PZ7.C67346 Mg 2003
[E]—dc21   2002013438

Printed in the United States of America 50

STEP INTO READING, RANDOM HOUSE, and the Random House colophon are
registered trademarks of Random House, Inc.

THE Missing Tooth

By Joanna Cole

Illustrated by Marylin Hafner

Alameda Free Library
1550 Oak Street

Random House 🏠 New York

Text copyright © 1988 by Joanna Cole. Illustrations copyright © 1988 by
Marylin Hafner. All rights reserved under International and Pan-American
Copyright Conventions. Published in the United States by Random House
Children's Books, a division of Random House, Inc., New York, and
simultaneously in Canada by Random House of Canada Limited, Toronto.

www.stepintoreading.com
Educators and librarians, for a variety of teaching tools, visit us at
www.randomhouse.com/teachers

Arlo and Robby were best friends.

They both rode green bikes

with horns that went WONKA-WONKA.

They both had ant farms

and horned toads.

They both liked

to trade baseball cards.

And they both <u>loved</u>

peanut butter ice cream.

Arlo said,

"I think we are best friends

because we are so much alike.

We even have a tooth missing

in the same place."

One day at school
their teacher said,
"Arlo and Robby,
look at you today!"

Arlo and Robby laughed.

They both had on

blue Robot Man shirts,

red pants,

and black sneakers.

Arlo put his arm around Robby.

He said,

"We match all over.

Even our teeth match."

Then Arlo and Robby

both smiled a big smile

so everyone could see.

Later Robby and Arlo
were playing checkers.
Robby said,
"Guess what?

My other front tooth
is loose."
He wiggled his tooth.

Arlo wanted to be
the same as Robby.
He tried to wiggle his tooth.
"I think mine is loose too,"
he said.
But it really wasn't.

"Let's make a bet,"

said Robby.

"If my tooth comes out first,

you have to give me ten cents.

If your tooth comes out first,

I have to give you ten cents.

Is it a deal?"

Arlo did not want

to make the deal.

But he said yes anyway.

They shook on it.

A few days later,

Robby went to Arlo's house.

They were going to trade baseball cards.

Robby had a Pete Rose card.

"I wish I had a Pete Rose card,"
said Arlo.

"Will you trade it?"

Robby shook his head.

"No, Arlo," he said.

"It is my best card.

I cannot trade it."

Arlo got up.

"I am hungry," he said.

"Let's not trade cards
anymore."

Arlo got two apples.

He gave one to Robby.

They sat outside together.

Robby bit into his apple.

He put his hand over his mouth.

"Look, Arlo!

My other tooth came out!"

Robby held out his hand.

The tooth was in it.

"Gee," said Arlo.

"That's neat.

But now we are not the same."

Robby did not seem to hear.

He saw Mr. Walker go by.

"Mr. Walker!" shouted Robby.

"I just lost a tooth!"

"Well, well,"
said Mr. Walker.
"The tooth fairy will be
coming to your house tonight!"

"With my tooth fairy money
I can buy more baseball cards,"
said Robby.

Then Robby looked at Arlo.

"Hey. I almost forgot.

We had a bet.

My tooth came out first.

You have to give me ten cents."

Arlo gave Robby the money.

But he was mad.

Robby was going to get money

from the tooth fairy.

Robby was going to get

<u>more</u> baseball cards.

And Robby already

<u>had</u> a Pete Rose card.

It was not fair.

Robby had everything!

Arlo went into the backyard.

Robby followed him.

Arlo began to swing on his tire.

"Can I swing too?" asked Robby.

"No," said Arlo.

"Let's play ball,"
said Robby.
"I don't want to,"
said Arlo.
"If you will not play,"
said Robby,
"I am going home."

"Hurry up," said Arlo.

"Don't keep the tooth fairy waiting!"

"You are mean,"

said Robby.

"I don't want to play

with you anymore!"

And Robby went home.

Arlo went inside.

He made a tower of blocks.

Then he pushed it down.

He felt as lonely

as his one space in front.

The next day,

Arlo did not say hello

to Robby.

At show and tell,
Robby showed
his tooth money.

He also showed
his box of baseball cards.
"I am going to buy
more baseball cards today,"
said Robby.

After show and tell,

Robby put away his baseball cards.

One fell out.

Robby did not see it.

But Arlo did.

Arlo picked it up.

It was the Pete Rose card!

Arlo wanted to keep the card.

He almost put it

in his pocket.

Then he looked at Robby.

It was Robby's card.

He would be sad

without it.

It was wrong

for Arlo to take it.

Robby was feeding the fish.

Arlo went over to him.

"Here, Robby," said Arlo.

"You dropped this."

"Gee, thanks, Arlo,"

said Robby.

Robby went and put the card
in his box.

"I am sorry we had a fight,"
Robby said.
Arlo nodded.
"Me too," he said.
Robby took something
out of his pocket.
It was ten cents.
"Take this back,"
said Robby.
"It was stupid
to make a bet."

Arlo thought for a moment.

Then he said,

"No. You keep it.

A bet is a bet.

Come on. Let's go play."

Arlo and Robby ran out
to the junglegym.

They climbed up to the top.

Arlo hung upside down.
His mouth bumped
on the bar.

Arlo sat up.

His hand was over his mouth.

"Robby, look at this!"

cried Arlo.

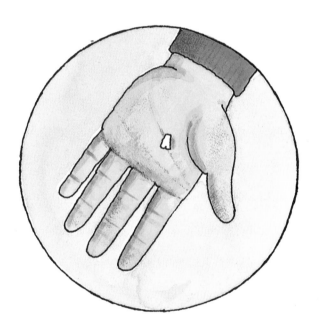

Arlo held out his hand.

There was a tooth in it.

"Now we have matching teeth again," said Robby.

"No, we don't," said Arlo.

Arlo opened his mouth.

The hole was in

a different place.

ALAMEDA FREE LIBRARY

Arlo and Robby

both smiled a big smile.

They did not

have matching teeth.

But they were best friends anyway.